One

KATIE sat on the hitching post in front of her summer camp bunkhouse. All five Wrangler-ettes were straining to read over her shoulders. She was holding a piece of Happy Trails Camp stationery. The scavenger hunt list had been scribbled on it.

"I think we ought to divide into two groups," Katie said. "And we'll divide the list in half, too."

Katie took off her hat and scratched her sweaty head. Wearing a cowboy hat was a great idea. If she didn't wash her hair for the rest of her life, who'd know? Especially since her hair was the color of a dirt clod. It looked dirty even when it was freshly washed and conditioned.

"Sounds good to me," Jill answered, chewing

on the end of her braid. "You're the *cowpoke.*"

Katie beamed proudly.

Katie Katz had never been in charge of anything in her life. Now she was the head of the bunkhouse for the two-week session at summer camp. Being cowpoke was sort of like being a team captain. And Katie planned to be the best cowpoke Happy Trails had ever seen.

"Okay, guys. Listen up," Katie said. "Lori, you and Anne take the top ten things on the list. Jill and I will take the bottom half."

"Does that leave me with the middle half?" Teresa asked.

If those words had come from anyone else but Teresa, Katie would have laughed. But she knew that Teresa wasn't joking. Teresa didn't know how to joke in English and Katie didn't speak Spanish. Sometimes she wished she could exchange her foreign exchange sister, Teresa, for a new model.

Katie turned to Teresa. "I guess you'll have to come with me."

The door from the neighboring bunkhouse squeaked open and Wendy and the Dude-ettes walked down the front steps. "Give it up, Wranglers," Wendy said in a snotty tone. "You don't stand a chance!" Wendy flipped her pony-tail over her shoulder. "The Dude-ettes are going to run circles around you!"

Katie hated the way Wendy tossed her hair all over the place. Wendy had blond hair, blue eyes, and a perfect tan. What a show-off!

Jill hooked her arm through Katie's and pulled her away. "Come on, Katie," she said, "don't let her get to you."

"She thinks she's so *hot*!" Katie groaned. "Just because she wears English riding britches and has a fancy leather crop."

Teresa followed Katie and Jill. "Hot?" she asked in a puzzled voice. Even though she'd been living with the Katz family for over a month, she hadn't gotten used to Katie's slang. It was a lot different from the English she learned at board-ing school in Buenos Aires.

"You know what I mean," Katie said. "She thinks she's *cool*."

"You mean she's hot and cold?" Teresa was trying to understand.

Katie rolled her eyes. "Oh, never mind!"

The three girls skipped down the path that traced the edge of the mare and foal pasture. It was Katie's favorite spot on the ranch. Sometimes she'd spend hours leaning on the fence watching the foals run with their tails whisking skyward.

Jill looked at the scavenger hunt list as they walked along. "A wild turkey feather?" she asked. "I've never seen a turkey with its feathers on. Have you?"

"Not in San Francisco," Katie answered, squinting into the sun.

Jill slapped herself on the hip, then took off in a gallop. "I'll race you to the lake!" she yelled.

Katie followed, yelling, "Ya-hoo!"

As she galloped up the hill, Katie remembered the Happy Trails Camp newsletter she'd gotten in the mail the week before camp started. It told about the camp's Rodeo Days at the end of the two-week session. The newsletter contained a line about Rodeo Days that especially interested Katie—"The winner will receive a silver belt buckle." She could just see herself with the shiny belt buckle around her waist. She just had to be the Rodeo Days winner!

Katie continued along on her imaginary horse, twirling an imaginary rope, and lassoing an imaginary steer. "Whoa!" she said at the top of the hill. She scratched her sweaty scalp and wondered what things she'd do at Rodeo Days to win the buckle.

Teresa had a hard time keeping up with Katie and Jill because of her roly-poly body. Katie thought that the only good thing about Teresa's fat was that it gave Teresa something to put into a bra. She also thought that Teresa's blubber was from eating too many tortillas and beans, even though Teresa tried to explain that they don't eat those things in Argentina.

Katie and Jill stomped through the prickly thistles with Teresa behind them. When they reached the clearing they saw campers from the "Broncos" and "Tackroom" bunkhouses.

Instead of looking for the things on the scavenger hunt list, the Tackroom kids were climbing into a teetering canoe. Three made it before the Broncos swiped the paddles. Katie watched the beginning of a playful splashing and kicking water fight. It didn't take long before everyone's Happy Trails T-shirts were dripping wet.

Katie returned her attention to the first item on the list—worms. She turned over a mossy green rock with the toe of her boot. Worms were something else they didn't have in San Francisco. They didn't have many horses, either, but that was one of the reasons Katie wanted to go to a dude ranch.

A few minutes later Teresa caught up, huffing and puffing.

"I have an idea!" Katie said. She draped her

arm over Teresa's shoulder. "I'm going to let you stay here by the lake and cool off. You can look for worms while Jill and I track down turkey feathers."

"Thank you, Katie." Teresa was still trying to catch her breath. "I'll find the biggest *serpe* you've ever seen!"

Katie didn't bother asking Teresa what *serpe* meant. She wanted to get out of there before Teresa figured out she'd been dumped!

Katie and Jill disappeared into the pine trees and headed up the rocky ridge.

"The only turkeys I've ever seen were wearing aluminum foil tents," Jill said.

"And little paper booties so their legs wouldn't burn," Katie agreed. "San Diego must be a lot like San Francisco."

"Yeah, I guess a city is a city," Jill said. "Maybe you can visit me sometime."

"That'd be great!" Katie smiled. "I'm really glad I met you, Jill. We speak the same language—unlike some people I know." She glanced down the hill in the direction of Teresa. "Teresa didn't even know what a sidewalk was. They call it *pavement* in Argentina. Have you ever heard of anything so dumb?"

"Maybe if she lost weight she wouldn't be so clumsy."

"Once a klutz, always a klutz," Katie said, shaking her head. "Hey, I know! When Dad goes duck hunting he puts wooden duck decoys in the water. Then he sits in his boat and blows a whistle." Katie stretched her lower lip until it looked like a duck bill. "*Quack!*"

Jill threw her head back and laughed. "I don't care if you are the best friend I've ever had at camp," she said between giggles. "I'm not going to act like a turkey."

Katie dropped to her hands and knees and made a gobble noise. Then she spread her fingers like feathers and wriggled them over her hip pocket. "Gobble! Gobble!"

Jill was bent over in laughter. "If anyone sees you, they'll think *you're* the turkey!"

13

"Gobble."

"Did you hear that?" Katie asked excitedly. "It's a turkey!"

Jill stuck her braid in her mouth and chewed skeptically. "Maybe it was an echo."

Then they heard it again—another *"gob-ble!"*

"That was no echo!" Katie said. Even Jill had to admit that it sounded like the real thing. Both girls strained their ears to listen.

"Gob-ble! Gob-ble! Gob-ble!"

14

Two

"I'LL bet we win the scavenger hunt." Katie whispered between gobbles because she didn't want to scare the turkey away. "The Dude-ettes would have never thought of acting like decoys!"

Now Jill was on her hands and knees, too. "I think it's coming from that tree," she said, nodding toward an old oak.

"How would it get up in a tree?" Katie asked.

"Maybe they fly."

"Yeah, that's why they have feathers," Katie giggled. "Now all we have to do is figure out how to get one!"

"*Gob-ble!*"

Katie and Jill crawled slowly toward the knotted oak tree. "Gobble, gobble, gobble," they said together.

"Talk about a couple of turkeys!"

Katie looked up to see Wendy and another Dude-ette sitting on a limb of the oak tree. "Gobble, gobble, gobble," Wendy mimicked, then roared with laughter. "I think we ought to stuff them with bread and cook them!"

Katie felt her face blush.

"Maybe they're not turkeys," Wendy howled. She grabbed a branch and swung down from the tree. "Maybe they're dodo birds."

Katie stood up and brushed the dirt and weeds off her pants. "At least we tried," she said. "I bet you didn't find a turkey feather."

"I didn't have to find one," Wendy said, pulling a feather out of her boot. She flicked it under Katie's nose. "I brought one with me. They had the same list last year."

"That's cheating!" Katie yelled.

Wendy smoothed her blond hair back. "It's not cheating," she said. "It's creative planning."

A loud whistle sounded from camp, ending the scavenger hunt.

"See you back at the corral," Wendy said with a grin. "When they announce the Dude-ettes as the winners!"

"What a lousy break," Katie said, watching the Dude-ettes scamper down the hill. "I hope the rest of the Wrangler-ettes did better than we did."

"I bet we can count on Teresa for the worm," Jill said.

"*Serpe*?" Katie thought out loud. "Do you suppose that's 'worm' in Spanish?"

"Maybe," Jill said. "I saw our counselor going over the list with her. They were translating some of the words."

"I'd never go to a country where I didn't know the language," Katie said. "They don't even call a bathroom a bathroom. What if you had to go and no one knew what you meant?"

Jill nodded. "She's so far from home. Two weeks at camp is about all I can take without getting homesick."

"You're right, but I just wish she wasn't such a

goody goody! She never does anything wrong."

Katie remembered when she first decided to come to Happy Trails Dude Ranch. She couldn't wait for her summer session to start. Now she wondered if she belonged at a dude ranch—not just because she was caught acting like a turkey and Wendy would never let her live it down. What really made Katie feel rotten was that she was going back to camp without all of the items on the list. She was the cowpoke and she'd let the Wrangler-ettes down!

"Come on." Jill yanked Katie's belt loop. "Let's head back."

The two girls skidded down the deer trail on their rumps and headed to the riding arena.

"Over here!" Anne shouted. She was sitting on the bleachers with Lori, two rows behind Wendy and the other Dude-ettes.

Katie and Jill climbed through the second and third rungs of the arena's fence. Chips of peeling paint flecked their blue jeans.

"How's it going, turkey?" Wendy asked Katie.

Katie ignored Wendy. She wished she had a giant bottle of invisible ink. Then she'd dip Wendy in it. *Presto!*—no more big mouth!

"How'd you two do?" Anne asked, as Katie and Jill plopped themselves down on the bleachers.

"Not so hot," Katie said. She pushed her sweaty bangs under her hat to keep them from stinging her eyes. "How about you guys?"

Ann unzipped her backpack and reached inside. "We got everything except the horseshoe nail," she said.

Lori looked around for Teresa. "Where's Teresa?"

Katie took a quick look around the bleachers. "Gosh, I don't know," she said. "We split up an hour ago."

The stable director, Wild Bill, stepped up on a bale of hay and shouted, "Listen up!" through a megaphone. He was wearing a baggy pair of denim overalls and a silly hat with a mule pin on it. Wild Bill was a real cowboy and Katie liked him a lot. So far he'd taught her how to bridle and saddle "Stinky," a caramel-colored mustang he'd rescued from a dog food pen in Nevada.

"Is everyone here?" Wild Bill asked.

Katie and Jill spotted Teresa at the same time. She was dragging an old feedbag down the dusty road.

"What's she got in that bag?" Jill asked.

"I don't know," Katie shrugged.

Bill turned his megaphone to Teresa. "What do you have in there?" he asked.

"I caught a worm," Teresa answered proudly.

"Let's have a look," Wild Bill said. Then he turned to the bleachers and chuckled. "The only reason I put worms on the list is because I want to go fishing tomorrow!"

Everyone laughed.

"And judging by the look of this sack . . ." Bill added, "you got a whopper!"

Teresa plopped on the haystack and untied the string around the sack. "Is it okay if my sister sees it first?" she asked Bill.

Katie groaned. She had a horrible feeling that Teresa was going to do something embarrassing.

Wild Bill patted the top of Teresa's head.

"Sure bet," he said, then turned to the bleachers. "Katie Katz?" he shouted. "Come on down!"

Katie thought Wild Bill sounded like the announcer on a game show. "Let's give her a big hand!" He stuck the megaphone between his knees and started clapping.

Everyone in the bleachers clapped, too—everyone, that is, except Katie. Instead, she slumped backward and pulled the rim of her cowboy hat over her ears.

"Come on, Katie!" Wild Bill urged. "This is no time to be shy!"

Katie hated getting up in front of crowds more than anything in the world. It all began in the third grade when she had to give an oral book report. Her palms had gotten sweaty, and she'd almost thrown up. Ever since then, her stomach churned up and down every time she had to be in front of people.

Katie swallowed hard. "Okay, okay," she said

reluctantly. She plodded down the steps, trying not to crush any fingers. Then she stepped *over* the piece of baling wire Wendy was using to try to trip her.

When Katie reached the platform, Teresa opened the sack. "I got the biggest *serpe* on the whole lake," she said. "You're going to be so proud of me!"

Katie looked at the bag. It was wet and dirty and had pieces of river grass sticking out of the creases. She put her hand over her nose and mouth. "Yuck!"

"What's the matter, Katie?" Wendy yelled. "Are you afraid of worms?"

Katie looked inside the sack, but it was dark and she couldn't see anything.

"She's not Katie Katz!" Wendy yelled again. "She's Scaredy Katz!"

Everyone laughed.

Katie was tired of Wendy's teasing, especially over a lousy little worm. She held her breath, closed her eyes, and quickly reached into the

sack. Her fingers brushed something long, coiled, and scaly.

"This isn't a worm!" Katie screamed. "It's a sn-sn-sn-ake!"

Three

TWO hours after lights out Katie was still tossing and turning in her bunk. She tried rolling on one side and tucking her knees under her chin, then on the other side and burying her face in her pillow. But nothing helped—her eyelids refused to shut.

"Katie, is that you making all of that noise?" Midge asked.

Midge was the counselor for the Wranglerette's bunkhouse. Katie liked her as much as she liked Wild Bill, especially the way she dressed. Midge didn't wear blue jeans and cowboy boots like the other camp counselors. Instead, she wore running shorts, tennis shoes, and leg warmers to protect her legs from the weeds. And instead of sleeping in a Happy Trails T-shirt, she wore a T-shirt that said, "When the going gets tough, the tough go shopping."

Katie also liked Midge's hair. It was thick, straight, and cut into a wispy bob. It didn't matter what Midge did—cartwheels or somersaults—her hair always fell back into place. Katie's own hair always seemed to be sticking out of place.

"I can't get that stupid snake out of my mind," Katie answered. "I know, I know. Wild Bill said it was a harmless king snake. But how was I supposed to know that? And how could Teresa do something like that?"

"The snake wasn't Teresa's fault," Midge confessed. "I accidently translated *serpe* for worm instead of *verme*. I'll give you three guesses what *serpe* means."

"Snake?"

"I'm sorry, Katie, but I've only had one year of Spanish in college. And vocabulary wasn't one of my strongest points."

Katie's mind wandered to the first time her mom brought up the idea of having a foreign

exchange student live with them. It was afte
read some article on "only children" in a psychol-
ogy magazine. At first Katie thought it was a
super idea because she always wanted a little
brother or sister to boss around.

But Teresa wasn't little. She was with the Katz
family less than a week and Katie knew it was a
BIG mistake. For one thing, Teresa never wanted
to do anything fun, like drop water balloons out
of the bedroom window. She wouldn't even snitch
a free ride on the back of a trolley car. Katie wondered if all of the kids in Argentina were such
goody-goodies.

Then her mom started saying things like,
"Katie? Why can't you be more like Teresa?"
Katie wished she could go back to the days when
her mom's biggest nag was, "Did you empty the
cat's litter box?"

"Midge?" Katie kicked off the sheets. "I have
to go to the bathroom."

"Better make it snappy," Midge said. "If we
don't get some sleep, we'll be worn out before the

sun comes up."

Tomorrow the campers would have their first day in the saddle. So far, they'd spent the first week at camp learning how to take care of and feed horses. They'd brushed the tangled manes and tails with curry combs and picked bits of gravel out of the hooves. Wild Bill even had them mucking manure out of stalls and polishing bridles and saddles with saddle soap.

"Psssst, Jill." Katie leaned over the top bunk and dangled her head upside down. "Are you asleep?"

Jill yawned. "What's the matter?"

"I have to go to the bathroom."

"Is that why you woke me up?"

"It's dark out there," Katie said, feeling around under her pillow for her flashlight. "And my flashlight battery's running low."

Jill sat on the edge of her bunk and rubbed her eyes. "Okay," she said.

Katie yanked on the bunkhouse door and Jill followed her into the warm night air. A three-quarter moon was shining on the empty flagpole. Its long skinny shadow fell on the Dude-ettes' bunkhouse.

"I'm sure glad I met you," Jill said. "Last year I got stuck in Wendy's bunkhouse. Ugh! Can you think of anything worse?"

"I'm glad I met you, too," Katie said. "I hate to say it, but I wish you were my foreign exchange sister instead of Teresa. She's such a goody-goody—and so polite! It makes me want to puke."

"Yeah," Jill said, nodding. "She does say 'please' and 'thank you' an awful lot."

"If you ask me, she's one sister too many!" Katie stopped in front of the Dude-ettes bunkhouse. "Did Wendy cheat last year, too, to win the scavenger hunt?"

Jill shrugged. "I wouldn't doubt it."

"That really burns me up," Katie fumed.

There were a couple of rumpled T-shirts and a bra hanging to dry on the Dude-ettes' hitching post. Katie knew the bra belonged to Wendy

because Wendy was the only Dude-ette with breasts.

Katie grabbed the 32-A cup bra and twirled it over her head like a lasso. "What do you think we ought to do with this?"

Jill giggled. "We could take it to the chuck wagon and fill it with grape juice."

"And put it in the freezer!" Katie laughed, snapping the bra. "Or," she paused, eyeing the flagpole. "How do you think Wendy would like it if we said the Pledge of Allegiance to her bra in the morning?"

"You wouldn't."

"Anything's fair in love and war. And when the Dude-ettes started calling the Wrangler-ettes turkeys, that was war!"

Katie handed Jill the flashlight, and Jill pointed the light on a piece of dangling rope. Katie knotted the bra strap to the flagpole and pulled on the rope until it was hoisted high into the air. Then she stood back and looked up. "I can't wait to see the look on Wendy's face!"

Four

THE next morning, Katie and Jill were in the barn getting ready to feed the horses. Katie separated a flake of alfalfa from the rest of the bale. Then she balanced it on her shoulder. The horses got a flake of alfalfa in the morning and a flake of oat hay in the afternoon. The first time Wild Bill said, "A *flake* of hay," Katie had imagined that a flake of alfalfa was the size of a corn flake. She thought the horses would starve to death. As it turned out, an average flake of alfalfa weighs about ten pounds!

Jill jumped from the haystack and followed Katie outside. "Did you see the look on Wendy's face when she saw her bra on the flagpole!"

"Her face looked like a ripe tomato," Katie

32

said, blowing a grape bubble. "I thought she was going to explode!"

"Do you think she knows we did it?" Jill asked.

"I hope so," Katie said. "I'd hate to think we went to all that trouble for nothing!"

The girls plopped down in the dirt to watch Stinky eat. "Mom would give anything for a vacuum cleaner with that kind of suction," Katie said. She took a stick of gum out of her pocket and offered half to Jill.

"No thanks," Jill replied, chewing on her braid. "It gets caught in my hair."

"We'd better tell all the Wrangler-ettes to be on the lookout," Katie said. She popped the new stick of gum in her mouth and chewed like Stinky until it softened. "Wendy and the other Dude-ettes will be after blood."

"Yours," Jill added.

"Maybe we could volunteer Teresa's," Katie said. "Hey, look who's coming. And look how she's dressed!"

Teresa was walking down the path on the other

side of the roping arena. She was wearing baggy pants and high-topped leather boots. Her coffee brown hair was slicked back underneath a flat-topped wide-brimmed hat.

"What kind of outfit is that?" Katie asked.

"It's a gaucho costume," Teresa said. "It belongs to one of my brothers."

Katie stood up to get a better look at the belt. It was made of foreign coins and was held together with a shiny silver chain. "Will this kind of money work in a video game?" she asked.

"The belt belongs to my grandfather," Teresa explained. "He sent it with me for good luck."

Sometimes Katie wished Teresa would dress like the other kids, so she wouldn't stand out. "I have an extra belt," she offered. "If you want to borrow it."

"Thank you." Teresa blinked, wide-eyed. "Did you want to wear mine?"

Katie wouldn't be caught dead wearing such a dumb-looking belt. Then the kids would really stare. "No, thanks," she said. "And you don't have to say 'thank you' all of the time. Just 'thanks' is enough."

"Okay." Teresa nodded. "Thank you for the advice. I mean thanks."

Even her thanks sound formal, Katie thought. She wondered if Teresa would ever sound like a normal kid.

"Buenos días," Wild Bill said in his raspy morning voice. *"Cómo está?"*

Teresa always beamed when someone spoke to her in Spanish. *"Muy bien, gracias,"* she said, smiling.

"Are the Wrangler-ettes ready for their first day in the saddle?" Midge asked, popping into the breezeway. This morning her hair was pulled into a high ponytail. Yesterday it was in a French braid. Her hair was the perfect length, thought Katie—short enough so it didn't make her shoulders itch and long enough to be pulled up.

Katie rushed up to Midge. "I was afraid you weren't going to make it."

Midge put her arm around Katie's shoulder.

"And miss my girls' first day in the saddle? Not a chance!"

Katie eyed Midge's red bandana. It was knotted around her forehead like a headband and tied under her ponytail. Katie loosened the knot in the scarf tied around her neck. She pushed it over her chin and nose and retied it over her forehead. That was one way to keep the sweat out of her eyes!

Anne and Lori skipped arm in arm into the arena. They were a matching pair, wearing their jeans tucked inside of their boots.

The bunkhouses had drawn straws earlier in the week to see which group of campers would ride first. Katie thought it was only fair that the Wrangler-ettes had beaten out the Dude-ettes, especially since the Dude-ettes had cheated to win the scavenger hunt.

Katie hooked the end of the rope to Stinky's halter and led him into the barn. She was so excited she could hardly put one foot in front of the other. Her legs were as wobbly as two rubber bands. The girls eagerly reached for the curry combs and brushes. It wasn't long before Stinky's mane and tail shimmered like spun gold.

Wild Bill stood in the doorway of the tackroom holding the saddle pad and saddle. "Good old Stinky," he said. "You finally get a chance to do your stuff." He dropped the saddle in the sawdust shavings and held up the pad. "Who gets the honors?"

The girls looked at each other, but no one answered.

Midge spoke up. "I think Katie should go first since she's the cowpoke."

"Okay, Katie," Wild Bill said. "Let's see if you can remember how to saddle a horse."

Katie took the pad and smiled weakly. "Thanks." She didn't want to go first, not with everyone watching.

The saddle pad reminded Katie of a giant piece of velcro because it was thick and scratchy. And if one corner touched the other it stuck together. Katie checked the pad for stickers or anything else that might be sticking to it.

Katie grunted when she tried to lift the saddle. "Why do they make these things so heavy?"

"Come on," Midge said. She smiled and patted Katie with encouragement. "You can do it!"

The barn lights were as blinding as the floodlights on her school's auditorium stage. Katie pictured Wild Bill with his megaphone shouting "ACTION" from a director's chair. The only thing missing was a drumroll from the sixth grade band. If only the other kids weren't there. Having an audience made her feel as if she were on stage.

"Remember what I taught you?" Wild Bill asked.

Katie thought back to the beginning of the week—the first week at camp when she learned to saddle the wooden sawhorse. "The trick is leverage, right?"

"You bet!" he said.

Katie grabbed the horn and lifted the saddle to her hip. Then she gave a giant heave-ho and tossed the saddle up—and over Stinky's back. It thudded in the shavings on the other side of his caramel body.

"Smooth move, cowpoke," Wendy said, standing in the doorway.

"I'd like to see you do better," Jill said, sticking up for her friend.

That was one of the things that made Katie and Jill best friends: Jill always stuck up for Katie.

"I guess I don't know my own strength," Katie answered, trying to control the blush stinging her cheeks.

"I could do better in my sleep," Wendy said. "And when it's my turn to ride I'll prove it!"

Teresa picked up the saddle and brushed the dust off. She carried it around to Stinky's left side and carefully placed it on his back. Then she buckled the cinch and took the stirrup off of the horn. "There you go, Sis," she said. "It's all ready."

Katie squirmed uncomfortably. She didn't like

Teresa calling her Sis, because she didn't want the other kids thinking she was related to a klutz. "Thanks."

"You're welcome," Teresa said. "Or should I just say 'welcome'?"

"No," Katie explained. " 'You're welcome' doesn't work the same as 'thank you.' In that situation, a simple 'don't mention it' is best."

"American is a very difficult language," Teresa said. "It's much different from the English they taught us at boarding school. But I'll keep trying. I'm a very good student."

Katie had to admit that Teresa did try. Maybe it wasn't even her fault that she was a blimpo. Maybe it was hereditary or something in the water in Argentina.

Wild Bill handed Katie the bridle. When she touched the chrome bit she remembered the time she put the halter on upside down. The lead rope stuck out of the top of Stinky's nose instead of hanging under his chin. Now *that* was really embarrassing.

"Maybe someone else would like a turn," Katie said, feeling an attack of nerves coming on. She hardly knew where she was or what she was doing. "How about you, Jill?"

"Gee, thanks!" Jill said, spitting out her braid. The tip looked like a paintbrush dipped in ink.

Katie watched Jill unbuckle the halter, slide it down Stinky's neck and rebuckle it. Jill put the bridle and the bit in his mouth and slipped the chin strap in place. Katie helped by sticking Stinky's ears in the eye-shaped leather holes and smoothing out his bangs.

Katie gratefully took the reins from her friend. "You did a good job," she said.

The whole procedure of brushing and saddling took about an hour. Wild Bill had his horse "Peso" ready to ride in less than twenty minutes. Peso was a big palomino that stood over sixteen hands. Katie learned about hands that first night around the campfire. Each hand is four inches— and that made Peso one big horse!

Wild Bill pulled the reins over Peso's head.

"Do you need a leg up?" he asked.

Katie eyed the stirrups. They were a lot higher off the ground than when they were on the sawhorse. Even Stinky seemed to be taller than normal with his saddle on. Suddenly, Katie had a horrible thought. What if the same thing happened to her that happened to the saddle? She could see it now. Up one side and over the other.

Katie walked next to Bill as they led their horses into the roping arena. Teresa, Jill, Anne, and Lori were walking along, too. Wendy and the Dude-ettes had climbed into the bleachers for a front row seat.

"Well, what do you think?" Wild Bill repeated.

"She's stalling!" Wendy shouted. "Scaredy Katz is afraid to ride."

If Katie had stepped into a bucket of water, steam would have hissed out of her collar. That's how she felt about Wendy and her stupid remarks. No, she wasn't afraid to ride. But if the arena had a trap door she'd make everyone disappear. Katie tried to ignore her audience. She lifted her leg into the stirrup, then grabbed the saddle horn and climbed the rest of the way up.

Midge and the Wrangler-ettes cheered.

"That's the easy part," Wendy shouted. "The hard part is staying on!"

Wild Bill swung up on Peso's back. "How's it feel?" he asked Katie.

Katie knew Wild Bill was talking to her, because she saw his lips moving. But she couldn't hear what he was saying. Her ears were plugged with the sounds of Wendy and the Dude-ettes stomping the wooden bleachers—and Midge and the Wrangler-ettes cheering *"yee-ha!"*

Katie tried to stand in the saddle to check the length of her stirrups but her knees locked. And when she looked down her head started spinning. It was the same feeling she had when she gave that oral book report. The teacher had called it "stage fright."

Wild Bill gave Stinky a gentle slap with his hat and Stinky trotted slowly around the arena. The more he trotted, the more Katie felt herself slip-

ping to one side.

"You didn't tell us you rode sidesaddle!" Wendy roared.

Wild Bill rode up to Katie. "Use the horn and pull yourself up," he said.

Katie tried to shift her weight, but it was no use. One of her boots had slipped out of the stirrup.

The last thing Katie heard was Wendy yelling, "TIMBER!"

Five

KATIE slid to the ground and teeter-tottered, trying to get her balance. Thank goodness her foot had found the stirrup in time for a semi-graceful dismount. Otherwise she would've fallen flat on her face. "Who's next?" she asked, flushed.

Lori hopped down from the fence and pushed her strawberry bangs underneath her cowboy hat. "Don't you want to ride anymore?"

Katie's knees finally unlocked and she stepped forward. "I wanted to make sure that everyone has a turn," she said.

"Well, you better get as much practice as you can. You have a week to practice before the rodeo," Wild Bill said.

Rodeo Days was planned for the last day of the two-week session at summer camp. The main competition would be between bunkhouses, but there were also individual events. The silver belt buckle was on display in the tackroom and Katie stopped to look at it two or three times a day.

"Are you going to give us a hint about the rodeo events?" she asked.

"Sorry," Wild Bill said. "They're a secret."

"Why don't you ask me?" Wendy spoke up. "*I* won the buckle last year."

Katie cracked her gum. "I'm not surprised," she said. "Do any of the events involve a turkey feather?"

Teresa cupped her hand around Katie's ear. "Don't forget about my grandfather's belt," she said. "I'll still let you wear it if you want to."

Katie wished she'd stop talking about her wearing the belt. Just the thought of parading around in a jingling chain of coins was more than she could take.

"Maybe you should wear your other belt,"

Katie suggested. "Your gaucho belt might get hooked on the saddle horn."

"Thanks for the advice," Teresa said, beaming. She was proud of herself for leaving the 'you' off of 'thanks.'

"Don't mention it," Katie returned.

Teresa's eyes widened questioningly.

Katie wished Teresa didn't have such puppy dog eyes. They reminded her of her neighbor's basset hound in San Francisco. It was impossible to stay mad at someone who had eyes like a basset hound.

"You say 'don't mention it' instead of 'you're welcome,' remember?" Katie explained. "And if someone asks you a stupid question," she paused to glare pointedly at Wendy, "someone from a neighboring bunkhouse, then you say 'give me a break.' "

"Give me a break," Teresa said.

"No, no, no. It's not supposed to sound like you're at a formal dinner party asking the hostess to pass you a break. You're supposed to sound bored. Maybe you should practice in front of the mirror and try adding a yawn."

Midge walked over. She plucked a stalk of alfalfa from a dark green bale and stuck it into her ponytail. "Does anyone know why Wild Bill named his horse Peso?" she asked.

"Nope," the girls said.

"Because he isn't worth more than a dollar!" Bill blurted, then laughed. The girls laughed, too. Especially Katie who thought Wild Bill's jokes were funnier than the riddles in her riddle book.

Each of the Wrangler-ettes took a turn riding Stinky around the arena. First they walked in a circle and then in a figure eight around two barrels. Afterward, Stinky was rewarded with a sponge bath and a scoop of horse pellets. Wild Bill led Stinky into a paddock next to the barn so he'd be easy to catch for the next day's lesson.

The following morning everyone was eager to ride. Wild Bill had promised to let them trot if they wanted to. They *all* wanted to.

"Who's up first today?" Wild Bill asked.

"How about Teresa the gaucho?" Wendy snipped.

"Yeah," Katie agreed. It was the first time she'd agreed with Wendy. It was a creepy feeling.

Teresa stood with her back touching Stinky's neck, then turned the stirrup. With a single jump she planted her foot in the stirrup and swung into the saddle. The day before she'd let Wild Bill give her a boost like all the other kids. Today she made it look like getting on a horse was the easiest thing in the world.

"How'd she do that?" Katie asked no one in particular.

Katie watched Teresa and Stinky as they moved at a quick gait. Teresa looked a lot different on Stinky than she had the day before— when they were walking around the ring. She sat straight in the saddle and held her head high. Katie was impressed.

"How'd she learn to ride like that?" Midge asked.

"She's really good!" Jill agreed.

Katie pulled the gum out of her mouth and wrapped it around her finger. "It beats me."

"I wasn't going to let anyone gallop on the first day," Wild Bill hollered. "But since Teresa knows what she's doing, I'm going to make an exception."

Even Stinky seemed to understand the compliment. He pricked his ears up and swished his tail. Teresa's smile stretched from ear to ear. "I'm honored."

"Isn't she great?" Anne nudged Katie with her elbow.

Oh, sure, Katie thought. *It's easy for her to be great. She doesn't care if anyone is watching or not. In fact, she probably likes having an audience.* Katie knew she'd be great, too, if there weren't so many kids around.

Katie couldn't help feeling jealous of Teresa, just like she couldn't help her feelings of stage fright. She wondered if stage fright were hereditary. Then she remembered the day her mom shouted across the grocery store, "Katie

Katz, get your buns to the checkout counter, now!" Then there was Katie's dad. Around the house he was dull and boring. But put him in front of a group of people and whamo! He was the life of the party. *No,* Katie thought dismally, *she hadn't inherited her stage fright.* There was no one to blame but herself.

Wendy climbed the gate and sat next to Katie. She spit on the tops of her fancy English boots and wiped them with her handkerchief. "It's obvious that you didn't get your sister's riding genes," she said.

"You'd better put on your glasses," Katie replied. "Because she's not even wearing jeans."

Wendy flipped her hair. "Very funny."

Teresa pulled up on Stinky and they trotted to the gate. "Who wants to ride next?" she asked.

Lori shook her head. "I'm not following that act."

Teresa didn't use the stirrup to dismount. Instead she swung her right leg over Stinky's mane and jumped down. Everyone rushed over, but Katie took her time, walking slowly. She decided she'd wait until she was alone with Teresa to ask her how she dismounted without using stirrups.

The questions were flying at Teresa from all directions. "Does everyone in Argentina have a horse?" "How old were you when you learned to ride?" "What kind of horses do the gauchos ride?" "What do their saddles look like?"

"That's what I'd like to know," Wild Bill said. "What does a gaucho saddle look like?"

Teresa explained in her best English. "A *sudadera* is a waterproof sweat pad that goes on the horse's back. It's covered with a roughly woven woolen blanket, then a piece of cowhide called a *carona.*"

Teresa's dark eyelashes fluttered. "The best part is the sheepskin that goes on top of the saddle," she explained. "It makes riding very comfortable."

"A saddle pad on top of the saddle?" Wild Bill took off his hat and slapped it against his saddle. "I'll be darned!"

54

Six

TERESA'S description of gaucho saddles was interrupted when the camp cook shouted, "Come and get it!" A rusty old cowbell punctuated Teresa's sentence with a clinkity-clink and was followed by, "First come, first serve!"

"I don't know about the rest of you," Katie said. "But I'm starving!"

"Me, too!" Teresa answered.

"Today's taco day!" Katie added. "We'd better hurry or the guacamole will be gone."

"What's guacamole?" Teresa asked.

"You know—mashed avocado. "It's that green stuff you put on tacos," Katie answered. She couldn't believe that Teresa would ask such a stupid question.

Teresa shook her head. "What's a taco?"

"You're from south of the border, aren't you?" Katie asked. "That's where tacos come from, isn't it?" She rolled her eyes, adding, "Give me a break!"

"Tacos come from Mexico," Midge said. "And Mexico is a long way from Argentina."

Teresa nodded. "Yes, it's a long way."

How was Katie supposed to know that? She'd gotten a $C+$ in geography and that was only because she made a papier mâché volcano for extra credit. The "plus" was for blowing Mom's talcum powder out of the crater. It made the volcano look like it was erupting and the classroom smelled like "Spring Blossom" for a week!

"You kids run along," Wild Bill said. "I'll put up the horses. The rest of you can ride after lunch."

Katie wanted to ride after lunch, too. But she didn't want to ask Wild Bill in front of the other kids. She didn't want to ride in front of them either. She wanted a chance to practice without anyone watching.

"You understand, don't you, Stinky?" Katie asked. She wrapped her arms around his thick neck and pressed her face against his hot, damp mane. "I wish you were all mine and I could ride you anytime I wanted to."

Jill walked over. "Now we'll have to stop calling Teresa a klutz."

"Yeah," Katie said, still feeling jealous. "She looks pretty good in the saddle."

"She's a cinch to win the silver buckle."

It was times like this that Katie felt like giving up. "At least it'd be in the family." Katie tried to smile, but her lips wouldn't curl. "You know what's funny? You have three sisters and a broth—"

"Ugh!" Jill blurted. "Don't remind me!"

"And you wish you were an only child, right?"

"Right!" Jill answered.

"I'm an only child and I wanted a sister," Katie

continued. "At least that's what I thought until Teresa arrived. Now I want to go back to being an only child. How do you figure that?"

"It's called the grass is always greener on the other side of the fence," Midge said, strolling over. "Have you heard that saying before?"

"Yup." Jill nodded. "It's one of Mom's favorites."

"Do you have any brothers or sisters?" Katie asked.

Midge untied her bandana and mopped the back of her neck. "I have thirty-four sisters."

"Thirty-four!" the girls repeated.

"Sorority sisters." Midge winked. "Are you two ready for lunch?"

"I'll be along in a minute," Katie said. "Save me a place."

Midge and Jill joined the other Wrangler-ettes, skipping down the road to the chuck wagon. Katie heard someone ask Teresa, "What kind of food do they have in Argentina?" A whole new bunch of questions followed.

Katie rubbed Stinky's muzzle, then led him over to Wild Bill and Peso. "Uh, Wild Bill . . . " She started and stopped. "Do you think, uh—?"

"What's on your mind, Katie?" Wild Bill asked.

Katie stared at the ground, twisting the toe of her boot in the dirt. "I was just wondering," she mumbled. "If maybe we could ride sometime. You know . . . just the two of us? Without the other kids around?"

"What's the matter with now?"

"Now? Really?"

"I remember my first rodeo," Wild Bill said, yanking Peso's cinch to the fourth notch. "I was so nervous I didn't know my own name."

"Really?" she repeated.

"Yup," he said. "Have you ever had butterflies in your stomach?"

"Boy, have I!"

"Well, I had buzzards," he chuckled.

Katie's hazel eyes grew bigger. "What did you do about it?"

"It's a long story," he said. "Have you got

a few minutes for me to tell you about it?"

Katie knew it would take the kids a while to line up and eat. "Sure," she said.

Wild Bill clasped his hands to give Katie a boost. "First, I try to think of something funny. Like the time I pretended my opponent had his pants on backward."

"Yeah?" Katie giggled. She followed Wild Bill's lead and trotted into the arena. "That's pretty funny."

"Part of the trick is pretending that I'm some place where I can't laugh. Like church," he said. "I concentrate so hard on *not* laughing that I forget about being nervous!"

Katie held the knotted reins tightly in her left hand. The armpits of her T-shirt were soggy and the bridge of her nose was sweaty.

"Do you think it'd work for anybody?" she asked.

"It's working for you," Wild Bill said.

"Huh?" Katie looked questioningly at Wild Bill. "What do you mean?"

"Look at you—you look like you were born in the saddle!"

"Really?" she asked, beaming. Stinky's front legs cut through the dusty air and churned it like a fan. The hot air felt good stinging Katie's cheeks. "I do, don't I?"

It was hard for Katie to believe that all she had to do to get over her stage fright was to concentrate on something else. Now she couldn't wait for Rodeo Days. Maybe she would have a shot at the belt buckle after all.

"I think it's time for this old cowboy to get something to eat," Wild Bill said, making their third loop around the arena. "What do you say?"

Katie didn't care if she ever ate again! She'd be happy to spend the rest of her life on Stinky's back.

"Shouldn't we cool them down first?" Katie asked.

"We'll give them a quick squirt with the hose," Wild Bill answered. "Then we'll put them on the walker."

Katie followed Wild Bill to the gate where they unsaddled the horses. This time she didn't have any trouble remembering what to do. She held the horses' halters tightly by their shanks while Bill hosed them off.

Katie picked up the boomerang-shaped metal scraper and drew the excess water off Stinky's back. Huge sheets of water ran off his flanks, making muddy pools in the dirt. Stinky shook his body and water flew everywhere.

"I don't know who's getting wetter," Katie laughed. "Me or Stinky!"

Seven

KATIE strolled into the chuck wagon in time to hear the campers bellowing the Happy Trails Dude Ranch song. It was sung in a round to the tune of "If I Had a Hammer." The Dude-ettes and the Wrangler-ettes were sharing a table and swaying from side to side:

> "At Happy Trails Dude Ranch,
> We swim in the morn—ing,
> We ride horses in the even—ing,
> All over this land."

Midge led the group by waving a knife and fork as if they were musician's batons. Katie joined in the chorus.

"We sing about the love between the campers
and the counselors,
At Happy Trails—Dude Ranch,
At Happy Trails—Dude Ranch,
At Happy Trails—Dude Ranch.

At the end of the song the girls whistled and cheered.

Midge tapped a glass with her fork to get the girls' attention. "Is everybody happy?" she asked.

The reply was an ear-splitting, "Yes!"

"How happy are you?"

"We're happy campers!"

Midge stepped on a chair to emphasize her last question. "And *where* are you happy campers?"

The girls exploded with, "At Happy Trails Dude Ranch!"

Katie joined her friends, eyeing the half-empty plates. "How were the tacos?"

"Tacos for lunch!" Wendy whined. "Hungarian goulash for dinner! Why don't they have American food?"

"Yeah," one of the Dude-ettes agreed. "Like pizza."

"Pizza's Italian!" Wendy said, bonking her on the head.

Katie rushed to the build-your-own-taco chow line and picked up a plate and a taco. The bowls were filled with sliced olives, tomato chunks, raw onions (yuck!), grated cheddar cheese, and shredded lettuce.

The best kind of tacos were those that Katie made herself. She'd start by spreading a layer of ground meat on the bottom of her tortilla and adding black olives, lettuce, and lots of cheese. The topping was a generous scoop of guacamole. And Katie liked three drops of tabasco sauce— not two drops or four drops, but *three* drops. Jill was the only other kid Katie knew who put tabasco sauce on tacos. No wonder they were best friends!

Midge stepped behind Katie at the food counter. "Don't you want rice and beans?"

"No, thanks," Katie answered politely, then

headed back to the table and looked for an empty place.

"P-U!" Wendy pinched her nose and stuck it in the air. "What've you been doing? Making mud pies with manure?"

Wendy and the Dude-ettes laughed.

Jill made room for Katie by stacking the dirty dishes and scooting them to one side.

Katie knotted the wet tail of her T-shirt. "I was helping Wild Bill give the horses their baths," she said.

"What's the matter?" one of the Dude-ettes snipped. "Wasn't there enough room in the tub for you?"

"I suppose I should thank you for washing Stinky," Wendy said. "Since I'm going to be the first one to ride after lunch."

"Who said so?" Jill asked, straightening. "The Wrangler-ettes are supposed to get their turn before the Dude-ettes."

Katie swung her other leg over the bench and her boot accidently swiped Wendy's thigh. A greenish glob of mud slopped on her shorts.

"And you put my bra up the flagpole, too, didn't you Katie Katz?"

"Who? Me?" Katie answered in a sickeningly sweet voice.

Wendy's cheeks billowed and her face turned bright red. She scooped a spoonful of guacamole and flung it at Katie.

"Oh, excuse me," Wendy chuckled. "But did *I* do *that*?"

Katie wasn't about to be outdone. She broke off a piece of her taco, stretched the neck of Wendy's T-shirt, and dropped it in. The crumbled shell soaked a giant grease spot through the Happy Trails lettering.

"I'm *telling*!" Wendy whined.

"We'd better get out of here!" Jill said, scooting back from the table. "Before one of the counselors shows up."

The rest of the Wrangler-ettes joined Jill in the dessert line. But Katie wasn't going anywhere. She was just getting warmed up!

"Don't just sit there!" Wendy ordered the remaining Dude-ettes. "Do something!"

The Dude-ettes did something all right. They scooted away from the table and joined Jill and the others in the dessert line.

Wendy pulled the hem of her T-shirt out of her pants. Crunched taco fell on the floor. "Eee-uuu!" She screwed up her mouth. "Disgusting!"

Katie was looking for something else to bombard Wendy with when Jill tapped her on the shoulder.

"I didn't know which kind of ice cream you wanted," Jill said. "So I brought a scoop of each."

Katie stared at the bowl and grinned devilishly. There were colorful scoops of chocolate, strawberry, and vanilla ice cream piled in a mound.

"Thanks," Katie said, taking the bowl. She thought ice cream would make the perfect dye for Wendy's perfect hair.

Katie picked up a spoonful of ice cream and flung it at Wendy's hair.

"How dare you!" Wendy cried and grabbed a scoop of ice cream from Katie's bowl. This time it was Wendy who grabbed Katie's shirt. Before Katie knew it, she felt cold ice cream dripping down her chest inside her shirt. Katie looked at her sticky clothes and made a face.

She looked up right into Midge's angry eyes.

Katie felt miserable. She couldn't wait to get out of her sticky clothes and into the shower. It was bad enough to lose the food fight with Wendy. What was even worse was making Midge angry. Even though Midge didn't punish her, the look on Midge's face was punishment enough for Katie.

Katie plodded up the steps and yanked on the stubborn bunkhouse door. A balloon was lodged above the jamb, tied in place with tangles of hair ribbon. When Katie walked through the door, the balloon wobbled. Then it fell and bonked her on the head. Molasses splashed everywhere, especially in Katie's hair.

"Ugh!" Katie sputtered through sticky brown lips. "When I find out who did this . . . I don't know what I'm going to do . . . but I'm going to do something!"

Eight

KATIE scooted sideways across the bunk's rumpled bedspread. "Ouch!" she said. "You're pulling my hair out by its roots!"

"Hold still," Jill answered. "I'm almost done."

It was four o'clock in the afternoon, which meant free time. Riding lessons and chores had been finished and it wasn't quite time for dinner. Most of the girls headed for the showers to wash off the day's horsey smells. Some went to the arts and crafts barn and others wrote letters to their parents.

Today, Katie and Jill were spending their free time flipping through a fan magazine. That's what gave them the idea to change their yucky hairstyles.

"I don't think the molasses is ever going to wash out," Katie said. "Cream rinse doesn't even soften it."

"Stiff is what's *in*." Jill continued to use a wide-toothed pick to comb Katie's hair. "I wish we had some styling gel for my hair."

"I have gel toothpaste if you think—" Katie said.

"Forget it!"

"Hey!" Katie said. "I have a can of whipped cream I've been saving for the next food fight. That's almost the same as mousse."

Jill giggled. "Go for it!"

Katie jumped to the floor, opened her trunk and dug through a wad of wrinkled clothes. She held up a can of whipped cream. "Here it is!"

Jill dangled headfirst from the top bunk. Katie popped the lid and squeezed a mound of fluffy cream into her hand, then ran her fingers through Jill's hair.

The door opened, and Midge poked her head inside the room. "You two have never looked bet-

ter," she said. "You'll be the stars of the show."

Katie and Jill flashed each other a what's up look. "What show?" Jill asked.

"You're being kidnapped," Midge explained. "You can come along voluntarily or you can be stuffed in a gunnysack."

Katie remembered the snake in the gunnysack and shivered. "You're kidding, right?"

Midge whistled. "Wild Bill?"

Wild Bill stepped in the doorway. He looked like a pirate, wearing a patch over one eye. Midge's bandana was tied around his forehead. "Are these two giving you trouble?" he asked, holding up two gunnysacks.

"Let's stuff them in the sacks and tie them to the back of the wagon," Midge joked. "Like the others who tried to get away."

"Others?" the girls repeated.

Jill jumped from the top bunk and followed Katie to the window. The Happy Trails hay wagon was parked outside, piled high with bales of straw. The counselor from the Tackroom bunkhouse was seated on the wagon's wooden bench. She was steadying a team of horses with a long pair of black reins.

"Be thankful you're still in your jeans," Midge said. "Otherwise you wouldn't get to ride horseback."

Katie eyed the kids in the back of the wagon. They were either wearing bathing suits or bathrobes. Wendy was one of those in a bathrobe. She was also wearing ducky slippers and her hair was a mass of pink sponge rollers. Teresa and the other campers were on horses.

"Seeing Wendy in curlers almost makes up for the molasses trick," Katie said, then quickly repeated, "almost."

"Wendy just got out of the shower," Midge said, laughing. "Most of the others were swimming in the lake."

Wild Bill shouted from the porch. "Let's move 'em out!"

"Where are we going?" Katie asked.

Wild Bill answered in a gruff voice, trying to

sound like an old pirate. "That's for us to know and you to find out."

Katie didn't really care where they were going, as long as she could ride Stinky. She'd been working all week on leaning into her turns when doing figure eights around the oil barrels. Even Stinky seemed to sense the excitement building up around the rodeo. There were only three days left!

Teresa was sitting on a big strapping bay gelding named Smokey. "I saved Stinky for you," she said, offering the reins to Katie.

"Thanks," Katie said. "I owe you one."

"One what?" Teresa asked.

"Oh, never mind," Katie said, then flattened her palm and held it out to Stinky. The wiry hairs on Stinky's lips tickled her hand. "I don't have any apples for you now, boy. Maybe later."

Katie stood on the bottom step of the bunkhouse and boosted herself into the saddle. Anne, Lori, and Jill were already on their horses. Lori was on a black mare named Chalkboard,

Anne rode a strawberry roan named Milkshake, and Jill was on Dimples, the dappled gray usually ridden by the Dude-ettes.

Midge swung into the saddle and whistled. "Wagon ho!"

Katie rode alongside Jill. "Do you know where we're going?"

Jill slapped Dimples affectionately on the rump. "Probably to initiate the new kids," she said. "We do it every year toward the end of camp."

"Yeah? What kind of initiation?"

"Last year we dipped the new dudes in tar," Wendy yelled from the wagon. "Then we rolled them in turkey feathers. Gobble, gobble, gobble."

Wild Bill and Peso led the way down the main road, beyond the bunkhouses and riding arena. They rode for another hour before turning onto an old cattle trail and winding around the base of Indian Rock. Wild Bill told stories about driving large herds of cattle to the local sales yard.

"You can't move 'em too fast or they lose too

much weight," he explained. "And weight means money at a cattle sale." Wild Bill took off his silly hat and held it over his stomach. "There were times when I thought my trail boss was gonna put me on the auction block. I'd have brought a pretty penny, don't you think?"

Midge trotted up next to Wild Bill and whacked him playfully with her reins. "Have you ever thought of going on a diet?" she asked. "Or maybe we should sign you up for an exercise class. What do you think, girls?"

Even though nobody could imagine Wild Bill in a leotard and tights, the answer was a booming "Yeah!"

"I haven't seen my toes in twenty years." Wild Bill chuckled. "I don't think I'd recognize them even if I could touch them."

"We're almost there," Midge said loudly. "Tie your horses to a tree and don't forget to loosen their cinches."

"It's about time," Wendy said, slouched into the hay. She'd taken the rollers out of her hair, but without a brush the ringlets resembled tiny springs. "This hay's been using me for a pin cushion!"

"Can't we ride a little bit longer?" Katie pleaded. "Just until dark?"

"You've been on horseback two hours," Midge reminded her.

"Don't forget we have to ride back," Wild Bill added. "By moonlight."

Katie and Stinky followed the wagon through the last grove of mesquite trees into a large clearing. A teepee of kindling was crackling inside a dirt pit, surrounded by a circle of river rocks. The rest of the camp's wranglers and counselors had arrived earlier and were busy unloading ice chests from the back of a truck.

Katie and Jill tied Stinky and Dimples to the branch of an old oak tree and headed for the chow line. Each of the campers was given a cleanly snipped piece of baling wire. A hot dog dangled off one end. Katie didn't bother with a paper plate or smothering a bun in ketchup or mustard. She liked her roasted hot dogs bubbly brown and crispy, right off the wire.

"I remember the first time we had hot dogs at your house," Teresa said. She sat on a hollow log next to Katie and Jill. "I thought your mother was really cooking a dog."

Katie nodded with a mouthful. "Yeah," she said, remembering. "And I told you it was a minced beagle."

"I should've known better," Teresa went on. "Since American hamburgers aren't made out of ham."

Wild Bill raked the burning embers while one of the counselors passed out small labeled jars. Some of the jars were empty and others were filled with a grayish powder.

Midge stood on a large boulder. "It's been a terrific two-week session and you've been a super group of campers," she shouted. "It's a tradition at Happy Trails Dude Ranch to send our campers home with a souvenir—a reminder of all the good times we've shared." She turned to Wendy.

"Would you like the honor of leading the returning campers around the fire?"

Wendy jumped to her slippered feet and retied her bathrobe. "Okay! All of you oldies but moldies," she yelled. "Line up and follow me!"

Wendy led Jill and the other old-time campers in a marching circle around the campfire. Everyone was singing the Happy Trails theme song.

> *"At Happy Trails Dude Ranch,*
> *We swim in the morn—ing,*
> *We ride horses in the even—ing,*
> *All over this land."*

Each girl emptied her ashes from the previous summer into the campfire. Wild Bill raked the hot coals off to one side, then mixed the old ashes with the new.

"It's time for the returning campers to take the hand of a new camper," Midge said.

Jill rushed over to Katie and pulled her off the

log. Now there were two rings of campers marching around the campfire. Everyone was humming the camp's theme song.

"It's time for everyone to fill the jars with fresh ashes," Midge said. "And fond memories of Happy Trails Dude Ranch."

Katie stooped next to Jill. "This is a neat idea," she said, filling her jar. "I'm going to keep the jar under my pillow at home. When I fall asleep, I'll dream of Stinky."

Jill giggled. "Or Wild Bill."

Nine

THE trail ride and initiation had been only three days ago. To Katie it seemed like another lifetime. It was the night before Happy Trails Rodeo Days, the day she'd been waiting for since she first arrived at camp. Yup, she thought. It's going to be another one of those tossing and turning nights.

Katie untangled her leg from the steamy sheets and tried not to think of the horseshoe toss or the egg race or any of the other events in the rodeo. Instead, she thought about paying Wendy back for the tar-like molasses that still globbed her bangs. After all, an entire week had passed and it was time to get even with Wendy and the Dude-ettes.

Katie's first thought was to do the same thing to Wendy that Wendy had done to her. Only Katie would fill the balloon with strawberry preserves or maybe catsup. *I wonder what Wendy would look like as a strawberry-blond? Katie giggled quietly.*

Itching powder in her hairbrush? Needle holes in her tube of toothpaste? Iodine in her sunscreen? Baby oil on the seat of her English riding saddle? Hey, that wasn't a bad idea! Then she'd slide up one side of the saddle and down the other—just like Katie the first time she tried to saddle Stinky. It was a good idea, but there had to be something better. She thought about it as she drifted off to sleep.

"Wake up!" Jill said, shaking the bunk. "Do you want to sleep through the rodeo?"

"Huh?" Katie asked sleepily. "What time is it?"

"Time to get up," Jill said. "Teresa and the others already went to breakfast. We're having

French toast today. Yum!"

Katie rubbed her eyes. Today was the big day, the day she'd been waiting for. At first she wanted to win the silver buckle so she'd have something to show the kids back home. Now there were other reasons for wanting to win the rodeo. She wanted to prove to Wendy that Katie Katz wasn't Scaredy Katz. *And* she wanted to prove it to herself.

"I can't believe today's really Rodeo Days," Katie said. She slid off the top bunk and wiggled into her boots. "It seems like we just started camp."

"Time flies when you're having fun," Jill joked.

Katie always slept in a Happy Trails T-shirt because it saved time getting dressed in the mornings. She raked a brush through her sticky molasses mop. Even though she'd been washing her hair and conditioning it every day for the last week, the molasses was just as sticky as the day the balloon burst.

"I wish Wendy had used marshmallows or

whipped cream," Katie said. "I might not look bad as a blond."

Marshmallows and whipped cream reminded Jill of food. Food reminded her of breakfast. "We'd better fill our tanks," Jill said with smacking lips. "We'll need all of the energy we can get for the rodeo."

The two girls raced out of the bunkhouse and down the steps. Katie knew it was important to eat a good breakfast before exercising. She also knew it was time to carry out her plan for Wendy. She checked her watch. It was eight-thirty and the rodeo was scheduled to start at ten.

Katie stopped when they reached the barn. "I'll be along in a minute," she said. "First there's something I have to take care of."

"I'll save you a place," Jill said and trotted off to the wagon.

At the beginning of the week Wild Bill had pulled names out of his hat to determine who would go first in the rodeo. Wendy was the first rider and Teresa was one of the last. Katie and

Jill were somewhere in the middle.

Katie ducked inside the tackroom and stood in front of the stacked saddle pads. There was only one pad used by Wendy—the fancy pad with interlocking lime green and burgundy riding crops. The other girls preferred the older Navajo blankets when riding a Western saddle. But not Wendy. She had to bring an English saddle to Happy Trails. Talk about a showoff!

"Wendy likes to be the star of the show," Katie said to herself, pulling out the fancy pad. "And what you see is what you get!"

Katie dug the tube of glue out of one pocket and a cocklebur wrapped in cellophane out of the other. She couldn't wait to see Stinky's reaction when Wendy stepped into the stirrup and the cocklebur tickled his side. She knew how she was when she was tickled. She would laugh so hard she could barely move! And she was sure Stinky would have the same reaction! He wouldn't budge! He wouldn't walk, trot, or gallop. He'd just stand there. And Wendy would lose the rodeo and look ridiculous while doing it. Maybe she'd think twice the next time she planned to bomb Katie Katz with a molasses-filled balloon.

Ten

KATIE was tiptoeing out of the tackroom when she heard Wild Bill in the breezeway. "I'll get the saddles," he said. "And you get the pads."

Who's he talking to? she wondered.

Katie ducked inside the room and looked frantically for a place to hide. The medicine chest with the vet supplies was big enough, but Wild Bill kept it locked. The only other hiding place was the big wooden bin that housed horse pellets. She lifted the hinged lid and crawled inside.

"How about a little side bet on the rodeo?" Wild Bill asked, stepping into the tackroom.

Katie smashed her bandana against her nose and tried to breathe as quietly as possible. She

didn't dare make a sound. If Wild Bill thought there was a mouse in the feed bin he'd head for the traps. A mouse in the feed bin? Oh, no! She hated mice more than she hated snakes.

Katie heard a second pair of steps. "Okay," someone said. "I'll take your wager." She recognized the voice of one of the young hands. "If I win, you paint the corral fences. And if you win, I'll varnish the rowboats. Deal?"

"Deal," Wild Bill agreed.

Katie couldn't wait to hear who they thought would win the silver buckle.

"I'll put my money on the kid with the English saddle," the hand said. "What's her name?"

Wendy! Katie thought.

"I'm going with the girl from Argentina," Bill answered. "She's a heck of a rider for her age."

Katie knew Wild Bill was right. Teresa was Happy Trails' best rider.

Then Katie heard the clanking of cinch buckles as they scraped the cement floor. The tackroom door slammed. *All clear.* She propped the lid with her head, careful not to let the lid slam, and climbed out.

Loose pellets had fallen inside Katie's boots and they crunched the soles of her feet. She didn't have time to shake them out, at least not now. There was no telling when Wild Bill would return for the halters and bridles.

Katie opened the door of the tackroom and quickly glanced down the breezeway. "Whew!" she sighed when the coast was clear.

The pellets gouged Katie's toes as she zoomed out of the barn and down the familiar dirt road. She ducked into one of the outhouses to empty her boots. There were six outhouses at Happy Trails and each had showers, sinks, and toilets. Today was the first time Katie had been inside an outhouse when there wasn't a line of chattering campers swinging curling irons by the cords.

Katie slipped into the last stall, leaned against the partition, and yanked off a boot. She was shaking pellets into the toilet when she heard voices. She squinted through the crack in the door and saw Wendy emptying a plastic bag of makeup on the counter. Tubes of lipstick rolled out along with blusher brushes, colored pencils, and a pair of tweezers.

"It was easy talking Teresa into trading places," Wendy said to her friend. "Especially when I told her she could use the fancy saddle pad."

Fancy saddle pad? The chrome handle on the toilet froze in Katie's hand.

"It's a lot better not going first," the other Dude-ette agreed. "Whoever goes first doesn't know what they have to do to win."

"Or *who* they have to beat," Wendy said, picking up the tweezers and attacking the row of stubble that connected her eyebrows. She grabbed one eyeliner pencil, then dropped it in favor of another. "Do you think I need a little more turquoise around the corners?"

"Try the frosted moonlight."

"I don't want to be the last rider, either," Wendy said. "I'll find someone else to trade with.

95

I want to end up with the best spot in the line-up!"

Katie glanced at her digital watch. It was nine forty-five. In only fifteen minutes Teresa would enter the egg race. In the egg race, the riders would trot in a straight line and balance a raw egg on a spoon. With a cocklebur in the saddle pad, Teresa was sure to look like a fool. Stinky wouldn't perform at all.

That was not the fate Katie wanted for one of her Wrangler-ettes, even if it was Teresa. After all, she was the bunkhouse cowpoke and very concerned about their image. The last thing she wanted was one of the Wrangler-ettes to end up looking like the rodeo clown. That was what Katie hoped would happen to Wendy.

Katie opened the stall door to a surprised Wendy. "Hi, guys," Katie said, hastily.

"You little sneak," Wendy said. "You've been eavesdropping! That's as bad as breaking and entering. I ought to have you arrested!"

"What about a balloon in the head?" Katie

countered. "That's assault with intent to commit bodily harm."

Katie didn't wait for Wendy to reply. She raced out of the outhouse to the roping arena. The bleachers were crowded with campers, counselors, and wranglers. Wild Bill was standing on the hay platform shouting through the bullhorn.

Teresa was already in the arena, holding a saddled Stinky by the reins. The crowd cheered for the first rider with enthusiastic whistles, claps, and stomps.

Katie sprinted to the bleachers, hoping to reach Teresa before she swung on top of Stinky. "Stop!" she shouted.

There was so much noise that no one heard her.

"Teresa Ruiz!" Wild Bill announced with gusto.

The polished black leather of Teresa's gaucho boot fit into the stirrup. Teresa climbed into the saddle and Katie realized there was nothing she could do except cross her fingers and hope for the best. Maybe Stinky wouldn't notice the cocklebur, or if he did, maybe Teresa's weight would take his mind off of it.

Katie watched as Teresa gently nudged Stinky with her heels. *Oh, no,* she thought, *here comes the laughter.* But then Stinky tucked his head between his front legs and kicked out with his back legs like a bucking bronco. Katie couldn't believe that the horse she was watching was Stinky. She didn't realize that a little sticker, smaller than the tip of her thumb, would make Stinky hop around like a kangaroo.

Teresa flew into the air and landed back down on the saddle with a *plop!* The color drained from her cheeks.

Katie closed her eyes and crossed her fingers. *Please,* she thought, *don't let anything terrible happen.*

The next time Teresa flew into the air she didn't come down on the saddle. All ninety-nine pounds thudded in the dirt.

Wild Bill was the first person to reach Teresa's side. "Someone get a stretcher!" he shouted.

Eleven

THE infirmary was a one-room wooden building on the other side of the chuckwagon. Katie had only been there once—to have a sticker dug out of her finger.

Katie thought to herself that it was a good thing that the nurse was in the bleachers when Teresa was bucked off. Katie would never forget the nurse's words, "Stand back! She needs room to breathe!"

"Room to breathe?" The words sent Katie into panic. "You mean she isn't breathing?"

That was over an hour ago. Now Katie was pacing back and forth in front of the infirmary. She couldn't think of anything except the look of horror on Teresa's face when she flew through the air. It was a look she'd never forget.

Katie didn't want anyone to get hurt, not even when she thought Wendy would get the cocklebur in her saddle pad. It was supposed to be a joke, something to make the other kids laugh.

The infirmary door creaked open. "Is she going to be all right?" Katie asked.

Wild Bill stepped out. "Yup. And she wants to talk to you."

"Oh, thank goodness she can talk!" Katie sputtered. "That means she didn't croak!"

"Croak?" Wild Bill chuckled. "What would make you think something like that?"

"Well, she wasn't moving and . . ." Katie said, running up the steps. ". . . And, oh, I don't know!"

"I'm going back to the arena and finish announcing," Wild Bill said. "And find out what's gotten into Stinky."

Katie stopped. "Check his saddle pad for cockleburs," she said.

Wild Bill raised an eyebrow and looked at Katie questioningly. "Cockleburs?"

"Yeah," she said, embarrassed. "It was supposed to be a joke."

"I don't like those kinds of jokes," Wild Bill said. "And a joke isn't funny when someone gets hurt."

No one knew that better than Katie.

Katie opened the door to the infirmary and waited for her eyes to adjust to the dim light. Teresa was lying on a cot with her ankle propped on a stack of telephone directories. Dirt was streaked across her cheeks, and her hair was a tangled mess.

"Hello," Teresa said. Her voice was low, but she didn't sound mad.

Katie scooted a folding chair to the side of Teresa's cot. "Are you all right?"

"Just twisted my ankle," Teresa said. "Nothing broken except my . . . how do you say it? Pride?"

Katie's eyes filled with tears. "But it wasn't your fault!" she said, sobbing. "I did it to get Wendy back for the molasses. I put a cocklebur in her saddle pad. And I'm so sorry! I didn't mean for anyone to get hurt. Will you ever forgive me?"

"Cocklebur?" Teresa asked, then laughed. "That is a good prank, yes?"

"That is a good prank, *no*!" Katie sniffed, then wiped her cheeks. "You could've been really hurt. Or worse!"

"That's not the first time I've been thrown off a horse." Teresa touched her ankle and groaned. "And it probably won't be the last."

"I'm sorry, Teresa. I really am. And I want to do something to prove it." Katie brushed the matted hair away from Teresa's cheeks. "Just say the word—I'll do anything."

Teresa thought for a moment. "Anything?"

"Anything!"

"Then go back to the arena and win the silver belt buckle."

"Ride in the rodeo?" Katie asked. "But I couldn't. Not now. Not after what's happened."

"My grandfather says it's important to get back into the saddle after you've been thrown."

Katie thought about that for a minute. "But I

wasn't the one who was thrown. You were."

"We're sisters aren't we?" Teresa's round dark eyes blinked. "You can do my riding for me." She unbuckled the coined gaucho belt and handed it to Katie. "Here, this will bring you luck."

Katie didn't understand how Teresa could be so generous, not after what happened.

"If I can't write to grandfather that I won the American belt buckle," Teresa continued. "I'd like to write that my sister won it."

Katie held up the belt and the coins glimmered in the dull light. "Okay," she agreed. "I'll do my best."

Katie arrived in the arena in time to hear Wendy's familiar whine, "It's uncivilized to do Western events in an English saddle. I'm going to tell Mother to insist on a change next year."

"What's with her?" Katie asked Jill.

"She's upset because she dropped the egg in

the egg race. She didn't do so hot in the other events either. Guess what? I think I'm tied for second place—that's a pair of horseshoe bookends."

"Super!" Katie said.

Wild Bill spotted Katie on the sideline. "Are you going to ride?" he asked.

Katie nodded. "Teresa wants me to."

Wild Bill turned to the crowd. "And now for our last rider. Let's hear it for Katie Katz."

"Yeah, Katie!" Jill shouted, climbing into the bleachers.

The same old butterflies filled Katie's stomach.

Wild Bill put the bullhorn down and spoke to Katie directly. "Remember," he reminded her, "think of something funny."

Katie imagined Wendy wearing her riding britches backward, but it wasn't funny. Nothing seemed funny with Teresa lying in the infirmary.

Wild Bill faked a hiccup. "Do you know what they call that?" he asked.

Katie shook her head. "No."

"A Wild Bill Hickok," he said, laughing. "Get it? Hiccup and Hickok?"

Yeah, Katie got it. She remembered reading about Wild Bill Hickok in her history book.

"What's the matter Scaredy Katz?" Wendy hollered from the stands. "Afraid you might get thrown, too?"

Instead of trying to think about something funny, Katie thought about Teresa. She concentrated on Teresa skipping down the infirmary steps, and the cheering faded into the distance. When she pictured Teresa swimming across Santa Margarita Lake, her butterflies flew the coop.

Katie climbed into the saddle. "It's now or never," she said to herself.

Wild Bill handed Katie the raw egg and spoon. "Good luck." Then he slapped Stinky on the rump.

Stinky took off in a fast trot across the arena. Katie knew she'd have to stand in the stirrups if she wanted to cross the finish line without dropping the egg. She put all of her weight on the balls of her feet and tried not to jiggle.

A few minutes later one of the wranglers was shouting, "We have a tie for the Rodeo Days egg race!" He clicked his stopwatch. "Thirty-six seconds."

The kids in the bleachers stomped and cheered.

Every time Katie started to get nervous she pictured Teresa eating a chili dog or slurping an ice cream cone. The remaining events were a breeze, including the rubber tire obstacle.

Katie patted Stinky on the neck after the last event. "Good boy," she said.

"Bravo!" Teresa shouted.

"Teresa?" Katie turned to see Teresa being pushed into the arena in a wheel chair. A wooden splint was taped around Teresa's ankle. It stuck straight out like the loader on Wild Bill's forklift.

"How did you do?" Teresa asked.

"Okay, I think," Katie said.

"Listen up," Wild Bill shouted from the platform. "It's time to announce the winners."

Katie and Teresa glanced at each other impatiently, then looked at Wild Bill.

"The winner of the Happy Trails belt buckle is—" He paused to hold up the buckle. "—from the Wrangler-ette's bunkhouse. Let's hear it for Jill Benedict!"

"Me?" Jill asked, surprised. "I won? *I really won!*"

Katie joined the others in congratulating Jill. She would've rather won the belt buckle herself. But since she didn't, she was happy for Jill. After all, Jill was a Wrangler-ette and Katie was their cowpoke.

"In second place," Wild Bill shouted, holding up the pair of horseshoe bookends, "is Katie Katz!"

Wow! Katie couldn't believe it. She won. *She actually won something!* She didn't win the belt buckle, but who cared? There was always next year.

"Congratulations!" Midge said.

"Thanks!" Katie said. She jumped off Stinky and handed the reins to Midge, then raced to the haystack. Wild Bill handed her the bookends and the megaphone. Katie didn't hesitate. She took the megaphone and hollered into the stands, *"Thank you everybody!"*

It was at that moment, standing on the haystack in front of the grandstand, that Katie realized she'd won more than the pair of bookends. She had learned to overcome her stage fright—that was a real victory.

Katie carried the bookends back to Teresa. "Aren't they far out?"

Teresa stared at the welded horseshoes. "Far out?"

Katie tried again. "You know. *Out of sight.*"

Teresa was still puzzled.

This time Katie didn't roll her eyes or make a *"tsk"* noise because Teresa didn't understand. "When we get home I'm going to teach you some good old American slang."

Teresa nodded. "And I'll teach you Spanish."

"I want you to have this," Katie said. She handed one of the bookends to Teresa. After all, it was partly because of Teresa that Katie had won them. "A souvenir from your American sister."

This was the first time Katie had called Teresa "sister."

"You'll be able to come back to Happy Trails next year, won't you?" Katie asked.

"I'll have to," Teresa said. "To get my grandfather's belt."

Katie had forgotten that she was still wearing the gaucho belt. "A trade? Yeah, why didn't I think of that? That's what Americans call *even Steven*."

About the Author

SHERRY SHAHAN is married and has two daughters. She and her family live on a horse ranch called Hidden Oaks in California where they breed and raise racehorses. Sherry considers herself an "adventurer at heart." Every year, she and her husband take a special trip to a foreign land and explore the countryside on horseback. They have traveled across Argentina, Kenya, New Zealand, and Hawaii on horses.

Sherry has been a writer for ten years. She gets her inspiration from everyday life with her own children. She also writes articles about her travels for magazines.

When Sherry is not busy writing or chauffeuring her children, she enjoys aerobics, jogging, and bicycling.